RE-RE THE RI...

WRITTEN BY:
TAKIYAH L. PROWELL

ILLUSTRATED BY:
JASMINE MILLS

PRINTED IN THE UNITED STATES OF AMERICA

FIRST PRINTING, 2020

WRITTEN BY TAKIYAH L. PROWELL

ILLUSTRATED/COVER DESIGN BY JASMINE MILLS

IDENTIFIERS:
LIBRARY OF CONGRESS CONTROL NUMBER: 2020912323
ISBN (PAPERBACK): 978-1-7353560-0-6
ISBN (HARDBACK): 978-1-7353560-1-3
ISBN (EBOOK): 978-1-7353560-2-0

PUBLISHED BY FAITH WRITE NOW, LLC
ST. LOUIS, MO
WWW.FAITHWRITENOW.COM

THIS BOOK IS DEDICATED TO MY FAMILY:

Mama
Joshua
Granny
Pa-Pa
Uncle Jerry
Uncle Robert

I LOVE YOU ALL. THANK YOU FOR SUPPORTING ME!
-Takiyah

Ta'Reena was very shy but enjoyed reading quietly.

Her big brother loved chess and her parents owned a bakery.

They all had fun together.
She always felt loved,
but they did not know exactly
how special she was.

Ta'Reena lived in St. Louis where all kids were amazing.

Some kids owned businesses while others could build cars, paint, and sing.

Ta'Reena could do things
no one else could.
But nobody knew her secret,
not even kids in her neighborhood.

She loved waking up early
to get ready for school.

Always first to wait on the bus,
Genius Academy was just that cool!

Genius Academy made learning fun.

Students played games, worked in labs, and banged on drums.

Ta'Reena loved everything about second grade because learning helped her grow in so many ways.

School meant more to her
than anyone knew.
It was where all
of her powers grew!

Yes, Ta'Reena had superpowers
of many kinds.

She could fly, shoot lasers,
lift buildings,
and read minds.

The more she read books,
the more powerful she would be.

One good thing was that
Ta'Reena really loved to read.

She carried a book
everywhere she would go.

She never knew when
she had to fight her foe.

Dr. No-Read was his name,
and he was really mean.
He wanted to destroy every
book the world had seen!

He wanted children to grow up
without learning anything,
so he could control their minds and
rule the world. Oh, how mean!

Dr. No-Read had built a strong machine that caused great fear. It was strong enough to make every book disappear!

There was a huge book fair
happening in town.
He was ready to go there
and tear every book down.

Ta'Reena was at recess reading her favorite book, then her mind began to tingle - she dropped it and looked.

Her Super Watch showed
Dr. No-Read at the book fair.
"He's going to do something bad.
I have to get there!"

Ta'Reena grabbed a hall pass
and ran to the bathroom.
She quickly gathered her gadgets
and put on her costume.

She flew to the book fair
faster than anyone could see.
"He's trying to stop us
from being able to read!"

She found Dr. No-Read and
his book-destroying machine.
"Stop it right now," she told him
as she fired laser beams.

"I knew you would come, but
you can't stop me," he said.
He blocked the laser beams
with the helmet on his head.

He did not know all that
she was capable of.
Turning invisible was one
of the powers she loved.

She went inside his machine
and ripped it apart.
"No! You always ruin my plans
from the very start."

The town cheered for
Re-Re the Reader.
She saved the book fair!

While Dr. No-Read
was locked away
from his evil lair.

No one at school knew Ta'Reena was gone.
She returned with ease,
making it back just in time
to visit the library.

Ta'Reena dashed through
the library doors excitedly
because reading made her powerful
and as strong as can be.

READING IS YOUR SUPERPOWER!

Did you know that when you read, you grow superpowers just like Ta'Reena? The more you read, the stronger your brain becomes. Reading can help you become smarter and do very well in school. You can be whatever you dream to be as long as you keep reading!

READING LOG

Every time you read, your mind gets to go on an adventure just like Re-Re the Reader! You can be a superhero too as long as you keep reading! Make sure that you read at least 20 minutes a day. Keep track of the books you read here.

1. Title: _____

   By: _____

2. Title: _____

   By: _____

3. Title: _____

   By: _____

4. Title: _____

   By: _____

5. Title: _____

   By: _____

6. Title: _____

   By: _____

MEET THE AUTHOR

Takiyah L. Prowell is a joyful and talented 8-year-old who enjoys reading. She has received various awards and recognition at school for her reading skills. Takiyah is a member of Young Biz Kidz, an organization based in St. Louis, Missouri that promotes entrepreneurship and financial literacy for children. She works as an assistant for her brother's business, JZ's Sweets. Takiyah loves to sing and dreams to become a nurse, veterinarian, and ballerina. She hopes that other kids will grow to love reading through Re-Re the Reader.

Made in the USA
Monee, IL
06 September 2020